PASTRY CHEF

MAKERS AND ARTISANS

JOSH GREGORY

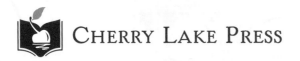
CHERRY LAKE PRESS

Published in the United States of America by Cherry Lake Publishing Group
Ann Arbor, Michigan
www.cherrylakepublishing.com

Reading Adviser: Beth Walker Gambro, MS, Ed., Reading Consultant, Yorkville, IL
Photo Credits: © xavierarnau/iStock.com, cover, 1; © Geoff Goldswain/Shutterstock.com, 5;
    © triocean/Shutterstock.com, 6; © Merla/Shutterstock.com, 8; © Miuda_21/iStock.com, 9;
    © New Africa/Shutterstock.com, 10; © NickyLloyd/iStock.com, 13; © wavebreakmedia/
    Shutterstock.com, 14; © Studio Romantic/Shutterstock.com, 17; © ferrantraite/iStock.com, 18;
    © Hamedgha/Shutterstock.com, 21; © dusanpetkovic/iStock.com, 23; © Oleggg/Shutterstock.com, 24;
    © TorriPhoto/Shutterstock.com, 27; © vincenzo patruno/Shutterstock.com, 28

Library of Congress Cataloging-in-Publication Data

Names: Gregory, Josh, author.
Title: Pastry chef / by Josh Gregory.
Description: Ann Arbor, Michigan : Cherry Lake Publishing, [2022] | Series: Makers and artisans |
    Includes index. | Audience: Grades 4-6
Identifiers: LCCN 2021007797 (print) | LCCN 2021007798 (ebook) | ISBN 9781534187252 (hardcover) |
    ISBN 9781534188655 (paperback) | ISBN 9781534190054 (pdf)
Subjects: LCSH: Pastry—Juvenile literature. | Desserts—Juvenile literature. | Baking—Vocational
    guidance—Juvenile literature.
Classification: LCC TX765 .G8165 2022 (print) | LCC TX765 (ebook) | DDC 641.86/5—dc23
LC record available at https://lccn.loc.gov/2021007797
LC ebook record available at https://lccn.loc.gov/2021007798

Cherry Lake Publishing Group would like to acknowledge the work of the Partnership for 21st Century
Learning, a Network of Battelle for Kids. Please visit http://www.battelleforkids.org/networks/p21
for more information.

Printed in the United States of America
Corporate Graphics

ABOUT THE AUTHOR

Josh Gregory is the author of more than 150 books for kids. He has written about everything
from animals to technology to history. A graduate of the University of Missouri-Columbia,
he currently lives in Chicago, Illinois.

TABLE OF CONTENTS

CHAPTER 1

Time for Dessert

The enormous, multilayered cake looks more like a sculpture than food. Colorful icing crisscrosses the smooth layer of white frosting covering each cleverly shaped cake layer. Atop the elaborate dessert are figures of a bride and groom made from spun sugar. You almost can't believe they are going to cut something that looks so amazing into pieces. But when you bite into your piece of the wedding cake, you find out that it somehow tastes even better than it looks. Who could have created such an incredible and flavorful work of art?

Pastry chefs are always looking to think outside of the box.

Pastry chefs must have really strong attention to detail.

Pastry chefs are cooks who specialize in creating desserts, from simple cookies to gigantic, decorative cakes. Dessert-making is a craft that people have practiced for centuries. But people have enjoyed eating sweet foods for even longer than that. Ancient people picked sweet fruits and gathered honey from bees. Eventually, they realized that the sweet juice of the sugarcane plant was a delicious ingredient. And about 2,000 years ago, people in India discovered that this juice could be turned into sweet crystals that were easy to store, transport, and use in cooking. Sugar rapidly grew to become one of the world's most desirable crops.

Edible roses are made from modeling chocolate or fondant.

Though it's a common food today, sugar was once very rare and expensive. Most people couldn't afford it regularly, if at all. But wealthy people in Europe served sugar-sweetened dishes at dinners as a way to show off to their guests. These foods were often meat or vegetables with sugary sauces or coatings, rather than the typical desserts we know today.

Pastry chefs create edible art.

Fruit tarts are a popular dessert topped with colorful fruit.

The word "dessert" comes from the French word *desservir*, which means "to clear the table." It was first used in the 1500s to refer to simple sweets such as fruit and candied nuts. These foods were often served at the end of large meals. Over time, dessert courses became more and more elaborate. Fruit and nuts were replaced with cakes and pastries. Chefs began experimenting with sweet flavors. By the 1700s, people in much of Europe and America were familiar with the idea of dessert, even if they didn't get to eat it very often themselves.

Today, sugar is no longer a scarce resource for most people, and desserts of all kinds have become common. You might have a chocolate chip cookie with your lunch or a small pastry with coffee in the morning. You're just as likely to find dessert on the menu at a fast food drive-through as you are at a fancy restaurant. Some desserts have also become ways to mark important moments. Think of the cakes served at birthdays and weddings, or the pumpkin pie that many people eat on Thanksgiving. Different cultures have their own dessert traditions, and families often have dessert recipes that are handed down from one generation to the next.

As good as old favorites can be, pastry chefs are always looking for new ways to make dessert exciting. And from restaurants to private parties, these tasty treats are always in demand.

Sweet Without Sugar

Today, traditional sugar from sugarcane plants isn't the only ingredient pastry chefs can use to sweeten their creations. Many plants produce sweet substances. This is why most fruit is naturally sweet. Corn syrup is a sweetener made from corn. It's especially common in the prepackaged desserts found in grocery stores.

Non-sugar sweeteners are made in laboratories. Many are designed to have fewer **calories** than real sugar. These sweeteners are often found in products such as diet soda.

CHAPTER 2

In the Kitchen

Pastry chefs aren't just cooks. They're also artists. They work hard to craft food that not only tastes delicious, but also looks incredible.

The first step of any pastry project is, of course, to decide what to make. In some cases, this might be as simple as consulting a recipe. But experienced pastry chefs are more likely to design their own desserts. They might start out to make a chocolate cake, but then put a unique twist on it. Or they might be tasked with making the perfect dessert to accompany an elegant meal. They must rely on their knowledge and experience to know what will and won't work. Even the most experienced pastry chefs aren't afraid to experiment and make mistakes, though.

Chocolate must be kept at the right temperature
to make it easy to work with.

Once the dessert is chosen, a pastry chef's next goal is to have the right ingredients on hand. Sometimes, this is as simple as making sure there is plenty of sugar and flour in the **pantry**. Other times, the pastry chef has to track down specialty ingredients. And even in the case of basic, everyday ingredients, a pastry chef might have specific needs. For example, getting just the right texture for a certain frosting might require a special kind of cream.

To make many batches, a pastry chef must use a large mixer.

The next step for most desserts is to mix ingredients together to create batter or dough. In most cases, chefs combine some kind of flour with sugar or another sweetener. They then mix the dry ingredients with eggs, water, or some other wet ingredient that makes everything stick together. It's important for the pastry chef to get the amounts of each ingredient just right. Dough that is too dry or too wet won't turn out right when baked. When following an established recipe, a pastry chef measures each ingredient by weighing it on a scale. Experienced pastry chefs might start out with basic measurements and then tweak them to get the results they want. They can tell just by handling the dough or batter how it will turn out once it's cooked.

Different desserts require the pastry chef to handle their mixtures in different ways. Bread dough containing **yeast** needs to be set aside and given time to rise before baking. Some kinds of dough must be rolled out on a flat surface and cut into pieces. Some need to be frozen or refrigerated before baking. It all depends on what the chef is trying to make.

Most pastry chef creations are baked in an oven. To make cakes, the chef pours batter into a shaped pan before baking. Cookies are spread out on baking sheets. Pies are carefully assembled in round dishes before baking. But baking isn't the only way to make sweet treats. For example, doughnuts are made by frying batter in hot oil. Creamy custard and pudding can be cooked on a stovetop.

Many desserts contain frostings, fillings, or sweet sauces. Making them might be as simple as mixing ingredients together in a bowl. Other times, chefs might do something more complicated, such as melt chocolate in a double boiler or whip egg whites into a foamy meringue.

Because desserts are often partially decorative, a pastry chef's work is sometimes much like sculpting. Some pastry chefs form decorative pieces out of materials such as **marzipan** or hard, sugary candy. With a little help from molds, sculpting tools, and food coloring, they can create figures of any shape and size. Want a cake covered in realistic, colorful flowers? Or a dessert shaped like your dog? A skilled pastry chef can probably make it happen.

Most desserts really come together at the end, as the pastry chef assembles the different parts. This might mean stacking layers of different sizes to create a tall tower of cake, or topping cupcakes

Pastry chefs will use piping bags to get details just right.

with decorative candies. A pastry chef might carefully spread frosting on the outside of the dessert, paying careful attention to keep a smooth surface. Or they might need a steady hand to write and draw on the dessert with colorful icing. Sometimes, the chef might use wooden skewers or other non-edible objects to hold

At some bakeries, workers must wear aprons and hairnets.

things together or serve as decorations. Once the finishing touches are in place, it's time to take a step back and make sure everything is just right. Some desserts may need to be transferred to other dishes for serving or carefully packaged for transport. All these things can affect the dessert's visual presentation as much as the dessert itself.

Of course, these are just some of the things a pastry chef might do in the kitchen. In reality, there are no limits. A pastry chef is free to use any techniques and ingredients they can think of to create mouthwatering, eye-popping desserts.

A Safe, Clean Kitchen

Like all cooks, pastry chefs regularly work with sharp tools and high heat. They need to be careful to avoid injuring themselves. They are also likely to get messy as they work. Most professional chefs wear a chef's jacket when they are cooking. It is easy to clean and has extra layers on the front to protect the chef. Some chefs also wear aprons.

A pastry chef's tools and workspace get messy, no matter what the chef is cooking. Wiping down surfaces and washing dishes are necessary to keep unwanted ingredients from getting into a dish. Cleaning up is also an important part of meeting health regulations.

CHAPTER 3

Sweet Success

It's not easy to become a pro pastry chef. It's hard work, and the job market is competitive. But for those who are truly passionate about desserts, it can be an extremely satisfying and rewarding career.

A few basic skills and talents can help aspiring pastry chefs succeed. Steady hands and an eye for detail help them manage tricky techniques. Pastry chefs also need both creativity and curiosity. The job rewards those who are willing to investigate and try new things. At the same time, pastry chefs need a strong understanding of traditional ingredients and classic flavors. It's hard to experiment effectively if you aren't already familiar with the basics!

Pastry chefs must be able to produce desserts that look identical.

The easy way to start on the path toward becoming a pastry chef is to make your own desserts at home. It could be as easy as asking a relative to show you how a favorite family recipe gets made. You could check out a cookbook from your local library or look up tutorial videos on YouTube. If you find that you have a knack for making sweet treats, you can improve your skills by taking a cooking class. They may even offer them at your school.

In school, it pays to focus on science, especially chemistry. You might be surprised to find how much baking is like a science experiment. Knowledge of different ingredients, how they react to each other, and what they do when heated or cooled are essential kitchen skills. You might also want to brush up on your business skills, including accounting and marketing. These will come in handy whether you become an independent pastry chef or work at a restaurant or bakery.

You don't necessarily need to go to college to become a successful pastry chef. An **apprenticeship** can teach you everything you need and help you connect with professionals in the food service industry. As an apprentice, you'll work as an assistant to an experienced professional pastry chef. At first, you might spend most of your time doing things such as cleaning or preparing ingredients. But you'll learn by watching the pros at work. Over time, your responsibilities will increase until you're making desserts on your own.

As an apprentice, you may help package desserts for customers.

Some pastry chefs want to learn as much as possible before kicking off their careers. **Culinary schools** are colleges that offer degrees in everything from food science to the study of wine. Most of them also offer programs for learning about baking and pastries. At a culinary school, you'll take classes and get hands-on experience. Some schools might help you find an apprenticeship as part of your education or offer connections to help you find a job after graduating.

Creating custom cakes is a big part of the business.

Talented pastry chefs have plenty of workplace options. Bakeries and cafés are packed with pastry chefs. High-end restaurants often have dedicated pastry teams who focus entirely on desserts. Similarly, you might find work at a hotel, resort, casino, or cruise ship. At catering companies, you could create desserts for all kinds of different events. Basically, pastry chefs are involved just about everywhere you could imagine eating dessert!

In your first job, you'll likely start as an assistant pastry chef. You'll take direction from more experienced chefs. You might be put in charge of making frosting or organizing the kitchen's supplies. You'll get more responsibility as you move up the career ladder toward becoming a head pastry chef. As you do, your daily tasks might shift to things such as developing recipes, creating schedules, or sourcing ingredients.

If you have the skills and are willing to put in some extra work, you can start your own business. This could be anything from making custom cakes in a one-person shop to opening a full-fledged bakery with employees. Owning a business generally means extra work hours and financial risks, especially when you're getting started. However, it can pay off in the long run if your business is a success. And best of all, you can be your own boss. Many pastry chefs and other **artisans** consider this one of the best parts of working in a creative field.

Tasting for Yourself

A good pastry chef is always looking for new flavors. What's the best way to expand your knowledge of sweet treats? Try as many as you can yourself! Of course, it's not very healthy to eat too much dessert, so you can't go crazy. Try to sample small amounts of dessert foods whenever you get a chance, though. A bite of cake or a nibble on a cookie can satisfy your curiosity without adding too many calories to your diet.

CHAPTER 4

The Tastiest Treats

Anyone can bake a simple cake or a batch of sugar cookies. True pastry chefs have always looked for ways to stand out in a world full of delicious treats. Centuries ago, chefs in places such as France and Italy often used ingredients you wouldn't expect to find in a dessert today. Imagine biting into a sweet, sugary dessert and discovering that it was made with eels!

Today's pastry chefs have a better idea of which flavors work best for dessert foods. But their creations can be wilder than ever. Some chefs go out of their way to create foods that look like one

A chocolate ball dessert with a caramel pipette.

thing but taste like something completely different. Want to try a flavorful pumpkin pie with filling that is crystal clear instead of orange? How about tiny balls of fruit that look exactly like **caviar**? Believe it or not, these are real foods.

Pastries come in many different forms.

People around the world eat traditional desserts that you might not find very often on menus at home. But even though they might seem strange to you if you aren't from these cultures, these treats are popular for good reasons. In Turkey, you can try a sweet, milky pudding that contains chicken. In Japan, buns and pastries are often filled with a sweet paste made from red beans. In Alaska, people have long enjoyed a frozen treat made of whipped animal fat and berries. It's a lot like ice cream!

Some pastry chefs try to outdo themselves by creating huge desserts. In 2008, students at a culinary school in Indonesia baked a cake that stood more than 108 feet (33 meters) tall, setting a world record. In 2020, a group of bakers in India set another record by creating a cake that was 17,388 feet (5,300 m) long. A huge crowd gathered to watch and then quickly devoured the cake within minutes of its completion.

Interested in becoming a pastry chef? Get out there and start baking! Take inspiration anywhere you can find it, whether it's from enjoying a dessert or looking at a sculpture. No idea is too wild. If you think of something that seems impossible, you might be the first to succeed.

Sweets on Screen

Cooking has long been a popular subject for television shows. Watching people prepare elaborate food can be both entertaining and educational. Today, many of the most popular cooking shows on TV are about desserts and baking. Some are competitions where pastry chefs are tasked with making desserts that will impress judges. Others show what life is like for professional pastry chefs working in restaurants or making custom cakes. While these shows might not always show a realistic version of a pastry chef's job, they are a great way to learn new things about baking and get inspired.

Craft Activity

No-Bake Cookies

Cookies are one of the simplest desserts a pastry chef can make, but that doesn't mean they aren't delicious. This recipe doesn't even need an oven!

SUPPLIES

- 2 cups (256 grams) sugar
- 1 stick of butter
- ¼ cup (32 g) cocoa powder
- ½ cup (118 milliliters) milk
- ½ cup (64 g) peanut butter
- 1 teaspoon (5 ml) vanilla
- 3 cups (384 g) rolled oats
- Waxed paper
- Timer
- Spoon

STEPS

1. Mix the sugar, butter, cocoa powder, and milk in a saucepan. Have an adult place it on the stove over medium heat.

2. Have an adult stir the mixture occasionally. When it starts to boil, start a timer for 1 minute. When the timer ends, turn off the heat.

3. Have an adult add the rest of the ingredients to the hot, melted chocolate mixture and stir together well.

4. Spread waxed paper on a cookie sheet. Use a spoon to place scoops of your batter on the waxed paper. Be sure to leave a little space between the scoops.

5. Let your cookies sit at room temperature for about 30 to 45 minutes. They should cool down and become solid. Enjoy them right away or store them in the fridge for later.

Find Out More

BOOKS

Labrecque, Ellen. *Chef.* Ann Arbor, MI: Cherry Lake Publishing, 2017.

Loh-Hagan, Virginia. *Bake Sale.* Ann Arbor, MI: Cherry Lake Publishing, 2017.

WEBSITES

Food Network—Recipes Kids Can Bake
www.foodnetwork.com/recipes/packages/recipes-for-kids/weekends-at-home/
recipes-kids-can-bake
These recipes are perfect for anyone who wants to start making homemade desserts.

U.S. Bureau of Labor Statistics Occupational Outlook Handbook—Bakers
www.bls.gov/ooh/production/bakers.htm
Check out official data about employment rates, average salaries, and more
for bakers.

GLOSSARY

apprenticeship (uh-PREN-tiss-ship) an arrangement where an inexperienced worker trains with someone more experienced

artisans (AR-tuh-zuhns) people who are skilled at working with their hands on a specific craft

calories (KAL-uh-rees) a measurement of the amount of energy contained in food

caviar (KAH-vee-ahr) eggs of a large fish such as a sturgeon

culinary schools (KUH-luh-nehr-ee SKOOLS) colleges that teach cooking and baking skills

marzipan (MAR-zuh-pan) a sweet, moldable material made from sugar, almonds, and eggs

pantry (PAN-tree) a room used for storing food and cooking supplies

yeast (YEEST) a microscopic, single-celled living thing used as an ingredient in most forms of bread

INDEX